CW00545184

A Broken River Books Original
Broken River Books
12205 Elkhorn Ct.
El Paso, TX 79936

Copyright © 2018 by Kelby Losack

Cover art and design copyright © 2018 by Matthew Revert
www.matthewrevert.com

Interior design by J David Osborne

All rights reserved. No part of this book may be repro-
duced or transmitted in any form or by any means, elec-
tronic or mechanical, including photocopying, recording,
or by any information storage and retrieval system, without the written consent of the publisher, except where per-
mitted by law.

This is a work of fiction. All names, characters, places,
and incidents are the product of the author's imagination.
Where the names of actual celebrities or corporate entities
appear, they are used for fictional purposes and do not con-
stitute assertions of fact. Any resemblance to real events or
persons, living or dead, is coincidental.

ISBN: 978-1-940885-48-3

Printed in the USA.

# THE WAY
# WE CAME IN

BY
KELBY LOSACK

BROKEN RIVER BOOKS

EL PASO, TX

*for everyone hustling*
*to get that bread*

*"Need ducats for real 'til the duffel get filled,*
*whether it's trapped in the rap or G'd a couple of deals."*

—"Due Rent" by Lojii & Swarvy

I

*I heard you scream before I opened my eyes. Nurses carried us to a blanket spread out on a cold, metal table. They set us next to each other and toweled the blood and birth cheese off our bodies. They weighed you in at half a pound heavier than me and then they shoved little tubes in my nostrils and kept them in there for a few days, until my lungs started doing the work on their own. I don't know what Moms was thinking, or what she said when she held her boys for the first time. Never thought to ask her.*

The gas it took to drive up to Huntsville the day you got out wasn't something I had the cash for, but I wasn't about to leave you hanging, even if I had a choice. I sat on the hood of the hoopty since it was too hot to wait in the car. Some guy with a gun and a badge and a crew cut slowed his walk when he came within earshot of the lo-fi trap music on my phone. Wouldn't take his eyes off me. I smiled, he didn't. Soon as he entered the prison, I plugged in my earbuds.

My palms were slick from wiping sweat off my brow and my shirt was starting to hug me. Thought about standing in the shade of the red brick walls, but that was closer to the inside than I cared to be.

You came out looking over your shoulder, keeping a steady stride, like if you didn't make it off the lot quick enough, they'd drag your ass back in.

I slid off the hood and you nodded a *what's up* and smirked, slapped my arm as you walked around to get in the passenger side. "Let's get the fuck out of here," you said.

I said, "Say no more."

The Elantra rattled to life on the lucky third turn of the key, then a couple back streets later, we were southbound on I-45, heading home.

For the first few miles, you just stared out the open window at clouds and the green blur of trees. Every time I glanced over, you were smiling.

You had more tattoos than I remembered you going in with. Triangle of three dots next to one eye, two teardrops under the other. Skeleton hands making a butterfly over your throat. Dollar sign on your neck. You were covered, all the way to your fingertips.

I said, "You went all Gucci Mane on me."

You turned the stereo down and said, "What's up?"

I waved a hand around my face and said, "The ink."

"Shit, five years is a long time to be bored, bruh."

"Bet."

You turned the stereo back up and looked at my phone plugged into the auxiliary. You read out loud, "X... x... underscore... zero – how the fuck you pronounce this dude's name?"

3

"I'm not really sure," I said. "Lot of rappers got weird names like that now. To stand out, I guess."

You shrugged, set the phone down. You leaned back in the seat and started bobbing your head, said, "Shit's flames, though."

You reached to turn up the a/c and nothing happened and I had to break it to you that it was busted. "That's why the windows are down."

You said, "Aw, hell. It's the wrong season for that."

"I'll get it fixed," I said. "We got a couple jobs this week, then I should be squared up with the landlord. We'll be straight after that, hopefully."

"I don't know, man. He might have to wait a couple days. I'm over here melting away." You shook my arm, said, "No wonder you so skinny."

I swatted your hand away and you poked at my rib-cage when I didn't laugh along with you and I swatted your hand again.

I said, "He's been waiting. This week is it."

"What, like, *it*? Like, pay up or get the fuck out?"

I nodded my head yes.

"Well, fuck." You thought for a minute, then said, "It'll be alright, though. Money ain't hard to get if you know where to look for it, know what I mean."

I shook my head, knowing exactly what you meant. "No, no, no," I said. "We're wrapping up a job this week, should have a check by Friday. It's just been a rough month."

You put an elbow on the door and scratched your chin. Went back to staring at trees and clouds. You sighed and said, "Saturn *is* in Capricorn," and I nodded my head like I knew what that meant.

When we pulled off the interstate to pump thirteen dollars of wishful thinking in the tank, you got out and said, "So let me see it," and of course I knew what you meant. I rolled up my left pant leg and you knelt down to touch the steel rod that ran from a plastic kneecap to down inside my shoe. You tapped on it with a fingernail. *Clink-clink-clink*. You stood, toothy grin wrinkling your face, and gave me a bear hug. The gas pump clicked. You kept squeezing me. The most I could do with my arms clamped to my sides was pat your waist. You let go and took a step back, pointed with two fingers at your eyes and then at mine. "I missed you being on this level." I set the pump in its cradle, screwed the gas cap on. "Yeah," I said, "fuck that chair."

We passed palm trees, liquor stores, machine shops, road construction. The air reeked of burning plastic and salt. The chemical plant almost looked like it was on fire, the way the top half of the sun glowed behind it, casting red and orange hues over its industrial silhouette.

We were back home, back in Freeport.

The house I was renting was a blue box sitting on cinders right next to the train tracks. The paint was bubbling off of the fiber cement siding. The yard was equal parts crunchy yellow grass and scalped to the dirt. Inside, the walls were lime green. I pointed at each of the three doors in the hallway, said, "That's you, that's me, that's the bathroom."

You looked around the living room. "Where's the TV?"

I said, "Pawn shop."

You said, "Ah, right, right."

I dropped to the couch while you moseyed around the kitchen, rummaging through cabinets, opening and closing the fridge door as if more food would magically appear. You asked if I was hungry and I said yeah and you asked where the food was and I said check the freezer.

Dinner was frozen chimichangas and tap water. You ate while pacing the room, picking photos up off of shelves, saying "haha, remember this?" with mouthfuls of food – cheese and taco sauce dripping between your fingers. The photos were all Mom's, so they were all taken when we were little kids. A snapshot with fold marks and yellow water stains of us riding bikes with training wheels. An under-developed pink photo of her – the angle tilted upward because it was either you or me who took it. In this photo, she sat on a porch railing in front of an azalea shrub, ashing a cigarette while blowing a kiss at the camera. You set the photo back on the shelf and swallowed. Licked your fingers clean. Said, "Man, it's a good thing you got these colorful walls. It's depressing as fuck up in here." You said this while touching the walls, and you said it in front of nobody, because I'd caught the mood and slipped off to the closet in your room, where – at the bottom of a box of clothes, tucked inside the case of those eyeglasses you were too stubborn to wear – there was a five-year-old stash of sour diesel I'd been holding onto.

We sat on the small square slab outside the back door and passed a glass pipe. A moth attacked the yellow porch light, casting chaotic shadows over our faces and arms. All of the constellations were out. I blew smoke towards the stars and asked if weed went bad and you said you'd never held onto it long enough to find out and then you took a hit and I heard it get sucked down inside you and you blew smoke out of your nostrils and coughed, passing the pipe back. You said, "Tastes fine to me." A train chugged past, its whistle wailing. We'd started with half an ounce in the bag. By the end of the night, we were smelling like skunks at a gas station. By the next morning, the baggie would be a crumpled plastic tumbleweed blowing down the road.

I woke to the sound of someone laying into their car horn.

Pieces of my leg were scattered across the floor, from the bed to the open door.

I found my phone tangled somewhere in the sheets. I texted Hector: *Hold up a sec*.

The horn outside quit blaring. Hector texted back: *Hurry up*.

I rolled off the mattress and scooted across the floor, slipping my prosthetic on piece by piece. First, I slid the sleeve on over my thigh, just above where my knee used to be. The socket that was shaped to look more muscular than my real leg was leaned up against the wall beneath a pot leaf tapestry. I strapped it on and hopped to the door, hand against the wall for balance. Found the steel rod and fake foot in the doorway. I screwed them into the socket and stood with two feet on the ground again.

There was no light in the crack under your door. I knocked. Heard nothing. I let myself in. You were sprawled out on your back, one side of your body hanging off the mattress. I reached down to touch your chest and shake you awake and you bolted upright and swung a left hook that caught me on the jaw. Knocked me on my ass.

"Sorry," you said, yawning/picking crusties out of your eye. "You can't do that shit. I just got out of prison, man, what's wrong with you."

"My bad." I popped my jaw. You stood and stretched and pulled me up to my feet.

My phone dinged and the horn blared as we got dressed. I wore my painter's whites: white T-shirt, white pants, white sneakers. You wore a black Dickies shirt with pearl snap buttons, ripped jeans, and khaki work boots. You said, "I did my share of wearing the same color shit every day."

Hector was still honking his horn when we stepped outside. I asked if he was trying to wake the whole god-damn neighborhood and he fired back with: "They're already awake, lazy ass."

We got in the van and Hector made the tires screech.

You sat in the back with the tools. I told Hector, "This is my brother."

He looked at you in the rearview, said, "No shit." To you, he said, "Nice to meet you. I did time, too. If you want to keep from going back, hermano, you have to stay busy. Work, work, work. Then go home and go to sleep. You stay busy, you stay out of prison."

Hector passed a car on a single-lane residential street where the speed limit was thirty. Paint rollers and nail guns and a weed-eater rolled around the back floorboard. Hector had all kinds of side hustles. He had a flip phone in the cup holder, another on the dash, and another buried between my seat and the console that wouldn't stop ringing. I dug it out and Hector shook his head.

"Don't answer that one," he said. "Fucking debt collectors."

I dropped the phone on the floorboard, let it slide back under the seat.

The job was a beach house down at Surf Side. It was a new build, still under construction. The house had plastic tarps where the doors and windows would eventually go. The tarps billowed and rippled like sails in the wind.

The owner's pickup truck was parked in the grass when we pulled up. The three of us carried the tools up the stairs. Buckets of primer, ladders, rollers, strainers. We parted the plastic curtain over the front door and saw the owner in the living room with a dripping roller in his hands, half the walls painted turquoise.

Hector dropped the ladder on the plywood sub-flooring and the clatter echoed. The homeowner flinched and turned to face us.

"Oh, hey, guys."

"What the fuck is going on," Hector said.

The owner's nervous smile faded. His sunburned skin glowed a deeper shade of red. "What the fuck is going on," he said, "is some fucking progress for once."

"We had a contract."

"I signed that three months ago."

"We've been juggling jobs. I told you this."

"Look, this is one you don't have to worry about anymore." And then the white boy said, "Comprende?" and Hector was done arguing.

He kicked the paint bucket over on his way across the room to throw hands with the white boy. Thick turquoise glugged out of the bucket and pooled on the floor. Hector knocked the guy against the wet paint on the wall and kept swinging.

You said, "This is looking like some jail shit." We set the tools down and walked back down the stairs to the van. The key was still in the ignition, as it always was.

We were five miles down the road when the cops sped by with their lights on, heading in the direction we came from.

I dropped the van off at Hector's and neither of us wanted to be the one to tell his wife, so we just parked it and left on foot. Hector's youngest daughter was riding her bike around the cul-de-sac. I thought maybe we should just let her know her daddy would be calling from jail again, but she had this content smile and I didn't want to be the one to take it from her. I waved. She rang the bell on her handlebars. You and I walked home.

You could load up a plate with home-cooked meals for four dollars at the senior citizen center, just had to show up by five and sit through the prayer. We wrote our names on the sign-in sheet and paid in ones and meandered about with the old folks while the volunteer cooks were finishing up in the kitchen. The floor was black and used-to-be-white checkered linoleum. One of the florescent lights flickered and hummed. Against one of the walls, draped over wooden ladders, were all these handmade quilts, plush and colorful. Paisleys/lady bugs/sunflowers. You felt one of the quilts and an old woman pushing a walker stood beside you.

"I made that one," she said. Pointing at several other quilts: "And that one, and that one. That one, too."

"Wow," you said, "that's amazing. I really fuck with these quilts, for real."

The woman's face beamed. She touched her chest and said, "Why, thank you."

A short, bald man who resembled a mole in an apron shuffled out of the kitchen to announce the food was ready. Fried black drum, okra, cornbread, mashed potatoes.

You pointed at the pitchers at the end of the food table, said, "What kind of tea is this?"

The woman behind the table cupped her ear, said, "What?"

"The tea," you said. "Is it black, white... green?"

"You've got sweet," she said, touching the lid of the pitcher labeled SWEET, "and you've got unsweet." She touched the UNSWEET pitcher.

You thought about it, ended up going with pink lemonade.

We sat at an empty table. The lady who made the quilts tapped your shoulder and asked if she could join and you pulled a chair out and she scrunched her nose up at you and sat down.

I moved food around with my fork. You mixed everything in with the potatoes and shoveled spoonful after spoonful into your mouth.

Because it was all I could think about, I said, "We need a grand by the end of the week."

I could see the potatoes in your mouth when you said, "That's it?"

I shrugged. "For the rent, yeah. Might be living with the lights off, but what else is new."

"That's easy money." You swallowed. "I know somebody, owes me a favor. Might have to get our hands dirty, but—"

"Yeah, well, I'm out of options at this point." I pulled my phone out and slid it across the table to you. "Call him."

"He don't keep the same phone for long. I'll have to hit him up on Facebook or something." To the quilt lady, you said, "This place got Wi-Fi?"

She threw a hand up in a shrug, gulping down some sweet tea.

I picked a tiny fish bone out of my teeth.

The quilt lady ran a finger from the corner of your eye to your cheek. "My grandson has one of those tear drops," she said. "His is a religious tattoo, is what he told me, something to do with when Jesus wept. What does yours mean?"

"Something else," you said.

We parked at McDonald's to use the internet. You bit your lip while staring at the blue and white screen on my phone. You said, "Forgot my password."

I said, "So, hit 'forgot my password.'"

You raised a hand and said, "Nah, nah, hold on, it'll come to me." You closed your eyes and rubbed two fingers on your temple. Mumbled something about a door and a hallway.

I said, "Are you for real—"

"Shhh."

"—doing guided meditation right now?"

You pressed a finger to your lips. Eyes still shut. You tilted your head as if straining to listen. To yourself, you whispered, "Ah, bet, bet." Then your eyes shot open and you typed something in the password box. You said, "Bingo." Then: "Damn, that's a lot of notifications." You shook your head as you scrolled, a smirk pasted on your face. You tilted the phone for me to see. "Bruh, look at all the females on my wall." You stuck your tongue out and went "heh-heh," said, "Shawties been missing your boy." You weren't lying. It was five years' worth of wish you were here and heart emojis and selfies. You said, "I'll have to hit these hoes up later." You posted a status update that read Finally free, whuss poppin? before you hit up your friends list, clicked on the name Tyrell Woods.

Tyrell saluted and winked at the camera in his profile picture – a spliff between gold teeth, face encircled by smoke. The first three posts on Tyrell's timeline: a selfie with a cash stack, held up to his ear like a phone; a three-second video zooming in on some sticky green-and-purple hydro; a video of him smiling at the camera before slamming a clip into an assault rifle and firing at liquor bottles from his back porch.

"Your boy's sloppy as fuck," I said.

"Nah," you said, "he's got all his shit set to private. Nobody but friends can see his shit."

I said, "Okay."

You clicked on the phone icon on his page and it rang for a minute and you didn't have it on speaker but I could still hear Tyrell's voice when he answered.

"Ohh, shit! Fresh out the pen! What the fuck is up?"

You grinned, said, "What's up, bruh." You flinched and held the phone out away from your ear. "You sound all glitchy and shit."

"That's because you called me on Facebook."

"Oh, yeah, that's on some phone bill bullshit. Hold up, I'ma climb on the roof, see if that makes it better." You crawled out of the window and pulled yourself onto the roof of the car and said, "Say something... Okay, cool, I hear you now."

The car tilted and bounced as you paced on top of it. I searched for something on the radio – all of the songs sounding the same, the lyrics blending together from station to station.

*"Is it too soon to/walk it like I/feel like a dangerous/country boys and girls/talk it, yeah, walk it like I/sueño que me sueñas en color..."*

I cut it off. Heard you say, "Hell yeah, just send me the addy. I'll give you the number to my brother's phone... A'ight, bet."

You hung up and swung your legs in through the window, slipped back into the seat.

"So, what's the deal?" I said.

"Don't worry your pretty head, child," you said, handing me the phone. "We'll have to put in some work, but Tyrell's going to give us a thirty percent cut off some shit."

"I need at least a stack in like, four days, or we'll be sleeping in this car."

You stared at me. Blinked. "So?"

I said, "So, how are we getting that much money?"

You said, "I just told you."

I started feeling pressure behind my eyes. I massaged my forehead with my fingers. "How much is it, exactly?" I said.

"What do you mean," you said, "the cash or the dope?"

I thought about it. "The work."

You held up a finger. "One day."

I was a little shook by that answer. Felt my eyebrows touch my hairline.

You laid a hand on my shoulder. "Selling drugs is easy, bruh," you said. "We'll be straight."

I nodded my head. "Alright."

The sky took on a dark shade of blue in the fading light of dusk. The golden arches sign lit up, reflected in the hood of the hoopty.

II

*Moms drove us to the high school so we could skate. The high school had stairs and handrails and we liked to pretend we were good enough for that to matter. We were thirteen. Moms was into photography. She had this box-shaped camera she'd copped from the pawn shop for a few bucks. Learned how to develop the film under a red light bulb in the bathtub.*

*Everyone would say it was the drugs, what killed her, but that's 'cause they weren't there. Truth is: some people got strong hearts, and Moms wasn't one of them. But I guess it's easier to blame the drugs. What nobody liked to hear was how she hadn't even hit the pipe that day, and her eyes were clearer than usual. She was smiling, crouching low to get the best angles of us popping ollies off the sidewalk. I said, "Watch me kickflip," and I flicked the board too hard, had to chase it across the parking lot, and by the time I'd turned around — carrying the board by the trucks – you were on the ground with her, holding her slack shoulders in your lap and crying, her head lolled over in the crook of your elbow. At some point, one of us must have called an ambulance, and then there was a funeral and boxes to be packed and we went to live with Aunt Beverly and our younger cousin Jocelyn.*

Jocelyn and Aunt Bev stayed in a Section 8 house a couple miles down the road. Walking distance, if we're trying to keep gas in the tank.

You ran your fingers along chain link fences. This dingo-looking dog jumped at you, barking and biting the air.

You held your hands up and said, "Whoa, my bad." Knelt down to eye-level with the dog, said, "My bad, a'ight."

The dog growled and paced the fence line. Barked once.

You said, "You right, you right. Are we cool?"

The dog licked his snout and turned tail, suddenly disinterested.

You said, "Cool," and stood up.

I watched all of this with a slack jaw.

You looked at me and said, "What?"

I shook my head. "Nothing."

We moved along down the street. You turned and waved to the dog, shouted, "Namaste!"

We came up to the complex. Grass up to our shins, bars over the doors and windows. We stood on the porch of the ninth unit and you rang the doorbell.

Two little girls – no older than nine – were having words over something in the parking lot.

Girl #1 [leaning over the handlebars of a bike with tassels and training wheels]: "You want to die?"

Girl #2 [turning on her heels to face Girl #1, slamming a Barbie doll on the pavement]: "Bitch, come see these hands!"

The door opened, and behind the bars and the screen, Jocelyn clasped her hands over her mouth to muffle a scream. She said, "Oh my god, you're so big!" She swung the screen and bars open and rammed her head into your chest.

You gave her a noogie, said, "What's up, cous?"

She said, "I'm so happy you're home." She turned to me and said, "What's up," gave me a side hug. To you, she said, "I see his ass all the time. How you been, though? Y'all come inside."

Jocelyn shut the door behind us, locked the deadbolt and the chain. The apartment smelled like childhood: dank weed, fried fish, and old lady perfume. Orange pill bottles and stacks of envelopes littered the kitchen table.

Aunt Bev was leaned back in a burgundy recliner, snoozing with her mouth open, making raspy gurgling noises.

I asked Jocelyn, "How is she today?"

"She called me a slut when I made her breakfast, so—" Jocelyn shrugged one shoulder, curled her lip, said, "—good?"

You said, "At least she's honest."

Jocelyn stuck her tongue out. Said, "Days when she's just a dick are okay. When she talks to dead people and sees spiders everywhere is when I get worried."

You tip-toed over to Aunt Bev. Gently rested a hand on her wrist and whispered her name. Her eyes fluttered open and she sucked in a breath. She blinked at you. Squinted behind her bifocals.

You said, "Hey, Auntie."

Aunt Bev rubbed the side of your head, felt the bristles of your prison cut. She said, "You," then got choked up, her eyes glossy wet. She cradled your chin in her hand, looked you straight in the face and said, "You have such a big forehead."

I pinched a thick strand of hair on my head and twisted it out – thinking I could stretch it, make it longer – crossed my eyes to see how low it hung down over my own large forehead.

You kissed Aunt Bev on the cheek and told her to never change.

We gravitated to Jocelyn's room.

On a vanity decoupaged with clipped-out body parts of magazine models, Jocelyn gutted a Swisher Sweet with a knife and dumped out all the tobacco, replaced it with some sticky hydro that had all these little flakes of purple in it. She licked the cigar paper and rolled the blunt tight.

You were picking up bracelets off her nightstand and sliding each one over your wrists, one at a time, until they were up to your elbows. You rotated your decorated arms, admiring the merchandise. Said, "How's the jewelry hustle going?"

Jocelyn had the blunt between her lips and was slapping a lighter against her palm. "It buys the weed," she said. "I started this cam girl show a while back, though." She sparked the blunt and toked. Let the smoke waterfall between her mouth and nostrils. "Shiiit," she said. "Talk about hitting licks. Thirsty niggas are quick to throw that bread." She passed the blunt to me and at the same time asked, "You okay?"

"What do you mean?" I said, taking a long drag and ashing on the dresser. Coughing up smoke.

"You're quiet," she said.

You pointed at me with the blunt I passed to you and said, "You want to talk about a thirsty nigga."

I said, "Fuck you," but I said it with a smile. The weed was loosening up my nerves, giving me the giggles.

Jocelyn asked you: "He told you about that one hoe?"

You said, "What hoe?"

I said, "I wasn't gonna tell him."

"Why not," she said, "that shit had me laughing so hard."

You said, "One of y'all has to tell me now."

Jocelyn looked at me with her eyebrows raised and I shrugged like, *go ahead.*

She said, "So he was fucking with this one girl – you know her, went to school with us, um – what's her name?"

"Keisha," I mumbled.

"Oh, bet," you said. "She was pretty cute."

"Still is," Jocelyn said. "Anyway, they were hitting it off, like, legit relationship status. They didn't even smash until the fifth time they hung out or something."

I said, "Third time."

She said, "Whatever, doesn't matter. So they finally smash, right—"

I said, "She asked about you."

Jocelyn said, "You just fucked up the punchline."

You touched your chest, said, "About me?"

31

"Yeah," I said, "right after we were done doing our thing, she looks over and says to me: 'So how's your brother doing?'"

You laughed. A cloud of smoke around your face. "That's actually kinda sad," you said. "You still got her number?"

I threw a pillow at you.

Jocelyn told you to quit being a bogart and you said "my bad" and passed the blunt back around.

"Hey, cous," you said, "you got those burners I stashed here way back?"

"What do you need guns for?" Jocelyn said.

"Just in case."

She exhaled. Passed the blunt and told me to kill it, so I did.

She slid the mirrored closet door open and shoved a pile of clothes off a combo lock safe. She spun the dial this way and that and it clicked open and she took out two Berettas – one glistening silver with a pearl handle, one all black – both serial numbers scratched off. She handed you the burners and tossed a box of ammo onto the bed.

You licked your teeth and grinned. Held both burners down at your waist, getting a feel for the weight again. Crossed them over your chest in the mirror. Mean-mugged yourself.

Jocelyn shut the safe, said, "What are y'all up to tonight?"

You aimed both burners at your reflection, said, "Going to a party."

.

We pulled up to a two-story pink-and-green beach house on pylons. You tucked the burner in the back of your jeans as you stepped out. Dropped your shirt tail to conceal it. I wasn't as used to carrying guns on the regular. Everything about it was uncomfortable: the bulge in my jeans, the coldness of the steel against my skin, the way it kept slipping as we ascended the stairs to the front door.

Stepping into the house was like crawling inside the chest of a living creature. Club rap blared from a midget-sized speaker in the living room, the beat carrying a pulse through the floor and up the walls. Blacklight bulbs in the ceiling fan turning everyone's skin different shades of purple. People everywhere – screaming in each other's faces to be heard. Folks played cards and toked spliffs at a round table, or they bobbed and thrashed to the distorted music, spilling drinks all over each other.

A box fan hummed in a corner. The scents of sweat, salt, and smoke mingled in the air.

We waded through the sea of bodies. A shout came from the kitchen and we both turned, saw Tyrell leaned against a countertop covered in foam cups. Gold chains/gold watch/gold grin. A glowing white smile beamed across your violet face. We pushed our way over and the two of you slapped hands and embraced.

"Goddamn," Tyrell said, "it's been a minute." He clapped you on the arm, said, "Whoo, big swol." Chuckled.

You said, "This is my brother," and he glanced at me over your shoulder and nodded like 'what's up' and I nodded back.

Tyrell asked if we needed a drink, but before we could answer, he'd set to double-stacking foam cups and uncapping lids. He dropped a handful of Jolly Ranchers in each cup. Threw some ice cubes in. Doused the ice and candy in cough syrup. Topped it off with Sprite. He handed the lean to each of us and raised his own double-stacked cups, said, "Cheers," and we each took a swig.

You tilted your head to say something in his ear without having to yell.

Tyrell nodded, said, "I got you." Took another sip. "Let's talk upstairs."

Tyrell began pushing his way out of the kitchen. You turned and laid your hands on my shoulders, said, "I'll be right back," meaning: *don't follow.*

I said, "How long's this shit gonna take?"

You said, "Just hang out for a while." Waved your arms around the room as you spun and walked in the opposite direction, shouting: "Enjoy the party!"

I slumped against the seashell wallpaper and watched you follow Tyrell up the staircase. The taste on my tongue was too medicinal, so I chugged the rest of the lean with my eyes clenched and poured up some more, cutting back on the cough syrup just a little, adding a couple more Jolly Ranchers. The volunteer DJ was too fucked up to do any good and everyone else seemed too fucked up to care. I wasn't that gone yet, though. The volume of the music had my skull rattling. I ventured to the back of the house and found a door leading outside onto the balcony. There was a plastic pink palm tree tangled in blinking Christmas lights. A couple making out. A dank-smelling pipe making its way around a circle. Someone snoring in a folding chair with their legs sprawled out. I leaned against the pinewood railing and sipped from the cup of purple stuff. The moon hung low over the rippling waves. In the distance, a dog chased a frisbee. I was content with admiring the twinkling reflections of stars in the ocean until some dude with fluttering glassy eyes staggered over, asking if I wanted to take a hit of this crumpled joint between his boney fingers. The smoke stung my nostrils and the aroma took me back. The shit was laced, had that fiery rubber smell – you know what I'm talking about – and it got me choked up with nostalgia, got me thinking about Moms. All I could do with the lump that rose up in my throat was shake my head and walk away.

I wiped my eyes with my wrist before heading back inside. Shot a glance up the stairs before posting up in a corner of the kitchen, where I stayed for a while – sipping the lean, trying to lose touch just enough to curb the anxiety. One of the candies in the cup rolled onto my tongue with the last drop. I poured up another. Drank it in a few quick gulps. Poured another. My head spun and my pulse decelerated.

A guy with short, purple dreads and round glasses that magnified his eyes was scratching his head and looking every direction, tip-toeing to see over people's heads. He was asking everyone if they'd seen someone named Remy. When he asked me, I said, "I don't know no Remy, man,

I'm sorry," then the man with purple dreads proceeded to open up and peek inside all the cabinets, calling Remy's name in a sing-song voice.

My teeth were starting to float.

I asked Purple Dreads if he knew where the bathroom was and he pointed without looking down the hall.

I rubbed my eyes after flipping the switch in the bathroom – my senses shocked by the artificial daylight glow of a regular bulb.

The tile floor was caked with sand. Towels kicked around over the footprints. Smudges on the mirror. Panties in the sink.

I set my cup on the counter and pissed.

That's when I saw the snake at my feet.

The python's tail was on one side of the toilet, its head on the other. It was a monster snake – body as thick as my arm. A split tongue shot out and licked my shoe. In my dizzy state, the snake appeared to have two heads, two tongues, and four beady, black eyes that I couldn't stop staring into.

I was frozen. Hypnotized. Shook.

Time stopped and I began to think I'd be pissing forever.

When my bladder was finally drained, I broke eye contact. Zipped and flushed with a quickness. Grabbed my cup of lean and backed slowly towards the door. The snake slithered across the sand-dusted tile and up the side of the tub. I turned the knob behind my back and almost ran into this chick in the hallway, who said, "You finally done in there? Jesus!" before shoving past me and locking the door.

My head continued to throb. The walls continued to vibrate. To my left was the living room, where everyone was getting throwed and enjoying themselves. To my right was a door at the end of the hall, cracked open with a sliver of pink light spilling out.

I made my way to the door and gently pushed it open. A woman in a white sundress sat alone on a sofa, shuffling cards. She pointed to a velvet chair in the corner. I dragged the chair across the room and sat facing the woman with the cards, a knife-scarred coffee table between us.

She asked if she could read my tarot and I asked if it was free and she smiled and said yes, it was practice for her, and I said, "Long as you're not taking my money, sounds cool."

She said, "Hold out your hand."

I held out my hand and she set the deck of cards in my palm, face down.

She said, "Shuffle them."

I moved several cards from the top of the deck to the bottom, then pulled from the middle and moved those cards to the top. I set the shuffled deck on the table.

She held up three fingers, said, "Make three stacks." An amethyst adorned her pinky ring. "Don't think about how you cut the deck," she said. "Just use your gut."

There were at least three things going on that made it easy to not think about. There was the lean in my system, yeah, and there was also the droning bass reverberating from down the hall, and then there was the shimmer in Tarot Girl's eyes, slightly obscured behind ringlets of black hair. I set a cluster of the cards to the left of the deck, then to the right.

She closed her eyes and extended a hand over the cards, palm down, hovering over each deck before drawing four cards at random. On the flip side of the cards were photos of naked women, their crossed-out phone numbers replaced by titles written in marker: Knight of Swords, Two of Cups, Queen of Pentacles, Death. The cards were also graffiti'd on. The woman cupping her tits on the Death card had a skull drawn over her face.

Tarot Girl caught my wide-eyed fixation on that one and giggled. "Don't worry," she said. "That card doesn't mean you're literally going to die. I mean, it could, but—" She shrugged. "Let's start from the first one." She began to explain the different interpretations of the Knight of

Swords, then the Two of Cups, but I had turned my ears back to the music blaring at the other end of the house. I didn't want to contemplate how Death fit into my life, not more than I already was, at least.

I took another sip of the lean. Picked up the Queen of Pentacles. The Queen wore red lingerie and chewed on her thumb nail. A crown was drawn crooked on her head.

I said, "Where did you get these cards?"

Tarot Girl blinked at me, her tongue between her teeth.

I said, "I'm sorry, I didn't mean to cut you off. They're just, um—"

"Vegas," she said. "I took a trip with some girlfriends last month. These calling cards were all over the place, just like, thrown on the ground and shit. I added the doodles, of course."

I said, "They're dope."

She smiled. Elbows on her knees. She asked if I wanted to dance and I said sure and she kept looking back at me as we made our way down the hall.

A shrill scream came from inside the bathroom as we kept moving past it. There was the sound of a door swinging open and smacking against the wall and I saw Purple Dreads bolt in that direction before shouting, "Remy! I been looking all over for you!"

40

I saw you leaned against a countertop in the kitchen, talking the way you do with your hands all over the place – a gaggle of intoxicated people entranced by one of your prison stories – and I told Tarot Girl to hold on a second.

I tapped some dude's shoulder trying to get by and he looked at me and then back at you, said, "Holy shit, you're like, fucking clones!"

Someone slapped him upside the head, told him not to say dumb shit, but that didn't stop everyone from looking us up and down when we stood next to each other.

You pulled me in with your arm around my neck. Peeked in my cup. "You're empty, bruh." You scavenged the littered counters for the syrup, the soda, the candies, the ice. Said, "Let me fix that for you."

I tried telling you: "I'm good," and: "Everything is tilting sideways," and: "Who's got the dough to share this much codeine?"

It was too loud to hear without looking directly at each other, though.

You handed me the refilled foam cup and toasted it with yours. I forced a smile and took a sip, glancing over my shoulder. Tarot Girl had disappeared somewhere in the crowd of bodies grinding up on each other.

You tapped me on the chest and waved me over to

a corner. You pulled a plastic-wrapped rock out of your pocket and bounced it in your hand. It was too big to wrap your fingers around. You tucked the yay back in and leaned close, said, "My pockets are full. Tyrell floated us seven ounces and gave us some customers for tomorrow. We get to keep thirty percent."

I said, "How much is that?"

You said, "Little over a stack."

I didn't know what to say, so I nodded and stared at the ground. The site of cocaine had set my heart to racing, and not in a good way.

You were smiling, of course. You loved this shit. Would have slipped back in the game even if I'd have had the rent money. For you, this was your true return home.

You grabbed my hand and swung my arm back and forth, using each swing to punctuate your words. "It... will... be... a'ight." You said, "I told you making money is easy." You raised your cup and said, "Hey."

I glared at you, but I also couldn't help but smile.

You said, "Here's to getting paid."

We toasted our foam cups and spent the rest of the night getting faded.

A blur of bodies bumping against each other.

Cups full of purple stuff.

Smoke clouds and strobe lights.

At some point, I passed out, and when I woke up on the floor the next morning, the first image that blurred into focus was a snake sticking his tongue out. Coming into focus behind the snake was Purple Dreads, who carried Remy coiled around his arm. He snapped his fingers in my face, said, "Wake up, nigga. Party's over. You don't live here."

The house was a different scene in the daylight. Everybody was gone, leaving only remnants of the night before.

A lime green bra on the card table.

A swept-up mound of colorful broken glass.

Empty foam cups being toppled over and blown about by the box fan.

I found you outside, lounging in the shotgun seat of the car with your shirt wrapped around your head, one leg hanging out the door.

I made my way down the steps and out to the car. Took the burner out of the back of my jeans and passed it to you to stick in the glove compartment. I said, "You couldn't wake me up?"

You said, "Do unto others, man. You know how I feel about that shit."

You'd found a pen and a scrap piece of paper and you were sketching a pair of hands –palms up – fingers bent

43

inward at the knuckles, on the cusp of curling into fists. I looked down at my own hands. Mimicked your sketch.

You said, "You ready to get this money, bruh?"

I turned the key in the ignition and you slammed your door shut.

You said, "Say no more."

You were saying something about lucid dreaming getting pretty freaky in prison, but I was finding it hard to pay attention with all the cocaine laid out on the dinner table.

We had a kitchen scale and some party favor bags from the dollar store and we were cutting up the yayo with baking soda, whipping it together in one of Mom's old mixing bowls, making a mess. We split the powder up into halves and eighths, give or take a couple grams.

My cell phone had a film of white dust on the screen. It sat next to the scale, Spanish trap crackling out of the tiny speakers.

You asked if I was fluent and I said, "My Spanish sucks. I just think it bangs."

The rapper said, "*Mira el movimiento de la muñeca.*"

You pinched the top of a baggie and spun the dope

inside so it twisted shut. We had a cluster of what looked like little plastic-wrapped balls of playdough on the table.

I said, "So when are we rolling out?"

You said, "Soon as we done."

The blue-and-white-striped sheets covering the windows were glowing. We had the lights off; nothing but natural illumination in the room. "But it's early."

"Yup. Fiends gotta cop they shit in the day, so they can party at night."

I jumped at the sound of knuckles rattling the screen door. You grabbed the burner off the table and for a few seconds, we sat motionless, staring at the front door. The rapper said, "*Me desperté sintiéndome como si estuviera en la luna.*" The second knock came heavier, more tenacious. I jumped again. You whispered, "Hide it," waving a hand over all the yayo. While you crept to the window to cop a glance behind the bed sheet curtain, I held the unzipped lip of a backpack to the table's edge and swept up all the contraband with my arm, then I shouldered the bag and spun around, ready to follow if you bolted, but you had tucked the gun in the back of your jeans and were reaching for the door knob, scratching your temple and shaking your head the way you do when you're trying to suppress a laugh.

You opened the door and a little girl stood behind the screen. She wore a green sash covered in patches and a matching green hat that was pulled over her braids. She pulled a wagon loaded with colorful boxes.

You leaned against the door frame with an arm over your head and smirked down at her, said, "What's up, little mama?"

"What's up," she said, "you want to buy some cookies?"

"I love me some thin mints," you said, "but I'll have to catch you another time."

The girl scout wasn't having it. She said, "We're raising money for a camping trip to Lake Texana."

"Good luck with that," you said. "Maybe try a better neighborhood."

"My mom said this is keeping me off the streets. You want me to grow up turning tricks?"

"Everybody gotta eat, shorty. Gotta snatch that paper how it comes."

The little girl's face contorted into a menacing glare as you said, "Bye-bye, now," and gently pushed the door shut.

We rock-paper-scissored in the car and I lost, paper versus scissors.

I said, "Damn."

You said, "Wait, what were you going for?"

"Doesn't matter," I said, "I'm not stoked about any of it."

We were parked in front of a small strip mall that contained a laundromat, tobacco shop, dollar store, and nail salon.

"How about this," you said, "I'll make the runs, you post up here. All you gotta do is wait for Tyrell's people to come to you. You got a burner just in case, but you shouldn't need it. I'll take your phone so you can call me if any shit goes down that ain't supposed to. You know your own number, right?"

I had to think for a second before I said yes.

I got out of the driver seat and you crawled over the console. Leaned the seat back.

I'd brought a box of laundry – figured might as well – and I was holding it on my hip when you chunked deuces and pulled out, saying, "Good luck."

I waved, said, "Yeah, you too," then went inside the laundromat to throw a load in the wash and wait for the fiends to show up.

The place stayed dead for the most part. I spun one of the folding chairs around and sat with my arms crossed over the back rest, my back turned to the floor-to-ceiling windows that faced the parking lot. Since you left me without a phone, I was stuck listening to the buzzing and clicking of the machines and staring at the walls, imagining patterns in the rough texture of the cinder bricks.

Customer #1 strolled in with no laundry asking if she could bum fifty cents for a wash. I looked over both shoulders, saw that Yoga Pants with her fresh blue fingernails had rolled up in a minivan. I told her, "Two hundred fifty," dipped into my right pocket, slipped her a half as she slipped me the bills. She left with a little more bounce in her step and – because I didn't know better – I thought, *damn, this shit is easy*.

A woman came in to pick up her clothes. She'd taken up four of the dryers and was carrying two baskets under each arm. She'd bring the baskets in, fill them up, dump them in her backseat, repeat. I held the door open for her as she walked back and forth. She didn't say thank you, but I didn't deserve it. I was just bored. Everything on this chick fit loose – her sweatpants, her two-sizes-up t-shirt, her face. Exhaustion had grabbed hold of the skin under her eyes and yanked down hard. On her final trek to the car, a couple quarters fell out of her sweatpants, jangled on the linoleum. She didn't notice. I let go of the door and when she drove off, I picked up the quarters. Both had landed heads up, a good omen. There were two arcade cabinets hooked up next to the clothes racks: *Mortal Kombat* and one of those racing games with the steering wheel controller. I dropped a quarter in the *Mortal Kombat* machine and tore that shit up as Raiden.

Customer #2 rode up on a ten speed bike. This skinny white boy was wearing one of those spandex suits like he was fucking Lance Armstrong or something. He asked for an eight ball. Asked it flat-out, just like that. I was still playing *Mortal Kombat* when he came up behind me and slapped three twenties next to the joystick. I said, "I don't know what you're talking about, man," and he said again, not even whispering, "An eight ball, brother. Some of that primo." I was trying to imagine what you would do if some dumbass fiend drawing way too much attention to himself came up practically announcing to the world that you were his drug dealer. You'd have taken his money, repeated you didn't know him, told him to fuck off, and he would've fucked off, 'cause people tend to not argue with you. I'm not you, though. I looked around the laundromat – caught nobody paying attention – then I snatched up the bills and dropped what he wanted into his gloved hand. I wanted to punch his dumb face when he clapped me on the shoulder and said, "Thanks, brother," but I just nodded and gave a weak smile. Smashed the game buttons harder than necessary. A voice growled, "Finish him!" and Scorpion reached inside Raiden's back and ripped out his skeleton. I was out of expendable quarters. The bell over the door rang and Lance Armstrong cycled off with his dope and I took a seat by the windows again.

An old lady with her hair in curlers hummed a gospel tune while folding.

A vagrant who'd been begging at the intersection shuffled in on concrete-spattered tennis shoes. The toes of his shoes were split open so it looked like they were yawning when he walked. The old lady humming gospels smiled at him as he passed. The vagrant spent a good long minute in the restroom and came out with beads of water dripping down his dreadlocked beard. He sat on a stool beneath a small analog television that hung from the ceiling. He watched a sitcom, laughing every time the studio audience laughed, and even when they didn't. His laugh was a raspy cackle that was often followed by a red-faced coughing spell.

I counted the black and white floor tiles.

I stared at the clock on the wall.

I tilted my head back against the warm window and closed my eyes.

Hum, cackle, hum, cough.

Customer #3 knew what the business was. Came in with his head low, pretended to check on one of the dryers. Or maybe he wasn't pretending. There were a lot of dryers running, even though the place was otherwise empty. Dude kept raking his arms with his fingernails like he was trying to dig something out of his skin. He sat in the chair next to mine and looked up at the mold and holes in the ceiling.

Whispered behind his hand: "Cop an eighth?"

Itchy had his arms crossed, some folded bills between his fingers. I dug a sack out of my pocket and crossed my own arms and we made the trade between our elbows. Then he dipped and I was bored again, alone amongst the whirring and clanking of unattended washers and dryers.

The vagrant was out in the parking lot talking to some teenagers, pointing at himself and then at the liquor store, working his own hustle.

I switched our saturated, dripping wad of clothes over to a dryer and just stood there for a minute, entranced by the tumbling laundry, my eyes rolling along with the drum. Hypnotized.

I got thirsty. That's how I ended up on the refrigerated aisle of the dollar store when the cops showed up. The clerk was a bedraggled, bloodshot mess, looked and smelled like he'd been living out of his car. We noticed the red and blue lights in the parking lot at the same time. Both of us stared paralyzed for a while before he turned and saw me standing there with a bottle of water in my hand, my heart in my mouth, dope in my pockets.

"There's an exit in the back," he said, "past the stock room."

I nodded in appreciation and staggered off in that direction, not even glancing over my shoulder until I made it out to the alley behind the strip. I saw the dumpster and didn't think twice. Dug all the yay out of my pockets in two fistfuls and tossed the baggies in with the trash. Shuffled down to the laundromat with trembling hands. My right leg throbbed with adrenaline, and from pulling all the weight, since my prosthetic was not the running-from-the-jays model.

There were a few people folding clothes or switching loads over. A gust of wind caught the metal door and slammed it shut behind me, which spiked my heart rate even higher, made me flinch. A couple sideways glances were shot in my direction, but for the most part, all eyes were on whatever was taking place outside. I crept up to one of the windows for a better view. The vagrant had caught the same paranoid wave I was riding and slipped back inside, too. I stood behind him and watched with the rest of the crowd.

The cop was out of her squad car, yelling something at a familiar face. He was still clawing at his arms as he paced around in a circle, the cop mirroring his every move. Itchy would walk this way, the cop would follow. He'd fake like he was going to bolt; she'd crouch into a sprint position and then catch herself, swipe the stray hairs from her brow. We couldn't hear anything from where we stood, but their faces said it all. Itchy was having fun keeping her on edge, making her chase him around. She was running out of patience, the veins on her head ready to pop off.

I asked what was going on, but everyone just shrugged. Nobody had caught the beginning of it. The cop drew a taser from her hip and someone said, "Ohhh, shit," and the vagrant chuckled and said, "Toast, motherfucker."

Itchy was still smiling, but now he was kind of cringing, too, the corners of his eyes pinched in anticipation. He said something with his arms stretched skyward and then he turned around and ran. There was a rapid series of clicking noises as Itchy's knees buckled and he bit the gravel. The cop followed the electric strings that caught Itchy in the spine. A pair of cuffs dangled from her finger.

My anxiety subsided. I took a swig from the stolen water bottle and strutted back to the alley, feeling good about my luck for a couple seconds, a feeling that vanished soon as I opened the back door to almost get clipped by the dump truck rolling between the buildings.

*No, no, no, no, no.*

That's all I could think. Just a whole lot of no.

I hung my head and bit my lip to keep from screaming as the truck's side forks lifted the dumpster in the air and tipped it over, swallowing up the cardboard boxes and black trash bags and – oh, shit, what did I do.

I walked in a trance back inside, fixated on the floor tiles and the hole between the sole and canvas of my shoe.

I stood in front of the dryer I'd tossed our clothes in. Took a minute to register that it was empty.

I sighed and felt several years of life leave my body. I don't know what's worse: fucking yourself over or getting robbed by someone else. I wanted to hit something so hard, it changed shape. Didn't matter what it was. Then I looked outside and saw the vagrant running up the street with a shopping cart full of fresh laundry.

The vagrant went *yeeee-hee-hee* like a happy lunatic. The wheels on his cart rattled and skidded over tiny rocks, but he scampered forward, unaffected by the crushed soda can I picked up and tossed at him, or by my shouting, "Hey! That's my shit!" The distance only grew between us the longer I tried to chase him. I limped after him for a couple blocks before my prosthetic started dragging and I was too winded and embarrassed to keep up.

I sat waiting on the curb outside the laundromat. Watched a fuzzy black caterpillar struggling to wriggle over the gravel and thought, *I feel that*.

Another fiend walked up, sort of timid and sketch. He was like, "What's up," and I just hooked my chin up at him – kept looking at the ground – then he gave me the once-over and was like, "My bad, cous, thought you was someone else," then he kicked rocks back to his Impala, burned out to go find another plug.

Awning lights were flickering on by the time you rolled up. I squinted in the headlights. You hung your head out the window and – even in the dark – I could see your smile, which made me feel worse.

I got in the shotgun and you said, "Bruh..." You shook your head slow – wrinkled forehead/crooked grin – you said, "What a day." You shifted into reverse, then lurched us forward by slamming your foot on the brake, holding it there, saying, "Oh," digging in your pocket and fishing out a thick roll of cash, saying, "peep this," dropping the roll in my lap. "I've got the rest of it in my shoe," you said, your hand on the back of my headrest as you turned to glance out the rear windshield while backing up. You giggled like a little kid. "Told you getting money was easy, man."

I was focusing on the texture of the cash in my hands, unrolling the bills and then rolling them back up, not saying a word until you nudged me with your elbow, said, "What's up? You look like you just got robbed or something." You giggled again 'cause you thought you were playing. When we pulled out of the parking lot, I still hadn't said anything. I don't know what scared me more: being homeless, being dead, or letting you down.

In the morning, we drove down to the beach. It was early and overcast and neither of us had slept. We walked to the vacant playground and I sat on a low-hanging swing and you put one foot on the merry-go-round and kick-pushed in slow circles.

A flock of seagulls wailed and pecked at the sand, hunting crabs.

"Could sell the hoopty," you said, "get a bike."

"Yeah, right," I said, "that car ain't worth but a couple hundred."

You kicked harder and lifted your foot off the ground as the ocean and the marriam grass and the chemical plant blurred around you. You spun for a few seconds and then buried your foot in the sand. Skidded to a stop. I stared out at the waves and thought about diving into them and drifting away.

You shook the sand off your sneakers and shrugged, said, "Could rob Hector. I mean, this is all technically his fault."

I said, "He's got kids."

You said, "We won't steal his kids, just his TV and shit."

I chewed on my lip, thinking about it – feeling sick to my stomach for thinking about it – said, "Nah."

I said: "Hector's good people."

I said: "I'd never do him like that."

You weren't pushing it, but I kept coming up with reasons, talking myself away from the idea.

A fisherman sat on the rocks of the jetty with his rod in one hand, beer in the other. A chihuahua sat on top of the man's cooler, panting.

You kick-pushed in slow circles again. I looked up at you spinning past and caught you looking at my leg – the one that wasn't a leg no more – and you caught me catching you looking at it and kept spinning.

You said, "You ever think about getting in the water again?"

I shook my head. "Not this water." I said, "I sometimes daydream about having a boat, taking it down to the river. There's no sharks in the river."

"There's gators," you said. "Always something out there that'd be quick to chew you up. That's anywhere, fam."

I poked the inside of my cheek with my tongue and shrugged. Toed the sand.

You said, "A boat would be dope, though."

A fuckload of Portuguese man o' wars – you know, those blue, bubble-headed jellyfish-looking creatures – had washed ashore among the soda cans and cigarettes. A group of kids walked up the beach, casually pulverizing the man o' wars with sticks, popping them like slime-filled balloons.

My phone buzzed. Tyrell again. My throat swelled. I said, "Your homeboy's been blowing up my phone."

You held your hand out and I tossed the phone and you caught it and answered.

"What's up."

I watched your jaw go slack, then clench.

I gripped the rusty chains of the swing to feel like I had a grasp on something. I couldn't keep my knee from bouncing and I could feel the bubbles in my guts and my chest caving in.

You didn't speak for a long time – just stood leaning over one of the handlebars on the merry-go-round, phone pressed to your ear – and when you finally did say something, it was short gibberish, like: "Sure, I feel you," and: "Yes, sir," and: "Where at?" Then you hung up without another word and chewed your thumbnail and spit a crescent moon in the sand.

You said, "I'ma kill Tyrell."

"What'd he do?"

"If he ain't dead yet, I'ma murk his ass, swear to god."

"The fuck's going on?" I said. "Who was that?"

You scratched your temple and ran a hand over your face. Said, "Apparently, Tyrell hit a lick on some other plug, and now motherfucker is out trying to get his shit back."

I said, "Oh," and then it was my turn to not say anything, but that's because I was having a panic attack. Saw the black dots in my peripherals. I didn't feel my stomach coming up until a small puddle of bile foamed up in the sand between my feet.

You were staring off, shaking your head, muttering some shit under your breath.

The kids with the sticks had taken to beating on each other and one of them wasn't taking it so well. I saw your lips moving, but all I heard was one of the brats shouting, "Quit being a pussy!"

# III

*We had this brindle pit bull named Gorgeous. Jocelyn had named him. She was eleven or twelve, so we must have been fifteen. It was summer and Aunt Bev was waiting tables in the day and mopping hospital floors at night and our restlessness had brought us to the train yard with a rattling backpack full of paint cans. Jocelyn was tagging an eyeball on the side of a rail car when a scrawny pit stuck his head out from behind the wheels. She dropped the can and went 'awww' and we abandoned spelling our names in graffiti script to pet the scab-covered tramp.*

*He followed us home and – between our pitiful, pleading eyes and Gorgeous shyly bowing his head – Aunt Bev couldn't say no. She saw the paint on our fingertips and said, "Maybe he'll keep you hoodrats out of trouble."*

The rest of that summer was like being in love. We took Gorgeous to the beach and threw sticks for him to fetch out of the foamy tide. I sacrificed my bike chain to make a collar and we took him on walks around the neighborhood, feeling like straight-up gangsters – gangsters who also made blanket forts in the living room and took turns cuddling with the dog.

It wasn't long after school started up again that everything went to shit. Jocelyn cried hard when Gorgeous went missing – an open gate the only clue as to what happened – but she cried even harder when he found his way back.

He'd been gone a month. We were shooting dice in the driveway – a game we'd seen in a music video, adopted with some rules we made up – when Jocelyn pointed a shaking finger towards the stop sign, her eyes already swelling. We looked and there he was: twenty pounds lighter, half an ear chewed off, and dripping from a gash in his ribcage. Gorgeous was limping his way toward us. We ran out to meet him in the middle of the road and he collapsed with all of our arms wrapped around him. You told Jocelyn to go get some water. Her shoes lit up as they slapped the asphalt. Tears flew from her face as she ran. When she was inside, you kissed Gorgeous on the head and said you were sorry. I flinched at the sound of his sharp yelp, his neck bones snapping. My hands were on his chest, so the last breath that rattled out before his lungs deflated – I felt that. You were trying to say something wise or comforting, but I wasn't hearing it. Of all the times that I wished I was you... in that moment, I was glad that I wasn't.

I retched and spit in the toilet. Flushed the clear foam.

You were using a blow dryer in the kitchen. I walked in and you cut it off and said, "What do you think?"

You were referring to the cling-wrapped torpedo of baking soda on the counter.

I shrugged. "I mean, yeah, looks like white powder."

You scratched the stubble on your chin. Stared at the fake yayo. Your eyes were red. We looked even more like each other than usual.

You asked if I was strapped and I said yeah and you sighed and said, "Fuck it." Put the fake yayo in a backpack. "Let's get this over with."

You cut three holes out of a Houston Rockets beanie – two holes for your eyes, one for your mouth. I dropped you off a block early and you stuck the mask in your back pocket and grabbed the burner from the glove box. Tucked the burner in your jeans.

We hadn't said anything the whole ride, and didn't say anything then. You paused, leaning in the passenger side window, and we shared this look that said a lot of shit neither of us had the words for. Then you slapped the roof of the car and took off down the street.

I wanted to roll the windows up to feel less vulnerable, but I didn't want to look more nervous than I already did by being drenched in sweat, so the windows stayed down.

You had said he'd be in an older model black Benz. I spotted it while pulling up, already waiting outside the payday loan center/Tae Kwon Do dojo. I parked on Alcario Rivera's passenger side and we made eye contact. Blank face. He tilted his head towards the shotgun seat, motioning for me to get in. It took everything in me not to cop a glance between the buildings, where you were hiding out, waiting. I got out of my car and into Rivera's. Set the brown paper bag on the console and then folded my hands together in my lap, conscious of how badly I was shaking. There was a gold watch in the cup holder that made me think of Tyrell.

Rivera unrolled the paper bag and let the fake cocaine slide out into his hand. He bounced the cling-wrapped powder, feeling its weight. "You did the right thing," he said, "bringing this back to me. You're not like your friend." He took out a switchblade to cut the plastic and taste the powder and I tried and failed to swallow the knot in my throat.

The shit that went down next seemed to happen all at once.

You ran out from behind the building, the makeshift mask covering your face, the burner in your hand. You touched the barrel to the glass of the driver side window. Rivera flinched and the knife and the baking soda fell to the floorboard and you opened his door and pulled him out by the shirt collar. Yelled at him to get on the ground, on the fucking ground, kept the burner aimed at his back as he lay prone on the faded blue square of a handicap parking space. His shoulder blades rose and then relaxed again. His eyelashes brushed the asphalt. Then you were digging in his pockets and I was scavenging through every compartment in the Benz, searching for anything of value. I should've been watching the rearview mirror, would've seen the pickup truck skirt up behind us, blocking both vehicles in.

You turned your attention to the driver of the truck, lost your shot when he ducked out and crouched between the cars. I didn't think quick enough to lock the door. That's how I ended up with a revolver kissing my ribcage.

The man ready to blow holes through my lungs if you didn't drop your gun had the bright eyes and soft face of a child. He wore the title "Pretty Boy" in cursive letters above his right eyebrow. He didn't blink.

You dropped the burner on the ground.

Pretty Boy told you to sit in the driver seat and you did and he told you to take the mask off and you did.

"Whoa," he said, looking between the two of us, "it's attack of the fucking clones in here." To Rivera, who was standing now, brushing the dirt from his slacks, Pretty Boy said: "You good, boss?"

Rivera answered by calmly walking over and spitting in your face. You turned your head and I saw the rage boiling up behind your eyes. And the fear – I saw that, too.

Rivera said, "Tape's in the glove box."

He said, "Throw these motherfuckers in the trunk."

They shoved us in the trunk in the sixty-nine position. Duct-taped our wrists and put strips over our mouths and even duct-taped my ankle to the steel rod of my prosthetic. Curled up next to each other like that got me thinking about the womb, thinking about how I couldn't stand nine months of your knees in my chest.

Six months, I mean.

We were going to leave this life the way we came in – neither of us ready to come out of the cramped darkness.

The ride was bumpy as fuck and the pop music coming from inside the car sounded like it was coming from underwater.

We were drenched in sweat and we were going to die with Bruno Mars stuck in our heads.

Remember learning how to drive? We couldn't see where we were going then, either. Too small to see over the wheel, so we learned how to drive by the feel of the road. I was always careful not to keep the wheel too straight, swerving this way and that, like I'd learned from watching Moms. Always thought of her driving all over the road as her version of rocking us to sleep. It usually did the trick, except for when she'd slam on the brakes and laugh hysterically at some shit we weren't privy to, reaching back with a hand that always shook, saying, "You okay back there, babies?" Then there was the time she didn't so much slam on the brakes as she did just let off the gas and sink into the driver's seat, hands sliding to her lap, head bobbing against her shoulder in rhythm with the tall grass blades slapping the rearview mirror. That might have been the first time we rock-paper-scissored for who would drive/who would navigate standing in the shotgun.

Whenever we'd have to pick Moms up by the underarms and ankles and sort of carry/sort of drag her gently as we could into the backseat — you remember how she smelled? It was like burning plastic, like when we'd use one of her lighters to pretend those little green soldiers had real flamethrowers.

That first time we drove the car out of a ditch, it was you standing in the seat, telling me which way to turn as I steered blindly with my foot reaching down to the pedal, my chin ready to get smacked by the airbag if I fucked this up and crashed us into something. I was too scared to take us all the way home, so you told me where to turn into a gas station parking lot and that's where we stayed until Moms woke up several hours later and I remember she was so proud of us, she gave us some money and said, "Go inside and get you some candy, and bring Momma a pack of cigarettes," but the clerk wouldn't let us buy cigarettes, so we came out empty-handed and she said, "Fine, I'll get it," and she adjusted her hair and bra strap and checked her teeth in the mirror then staggered inside and when she came back out, she didn't have any candy, but we didn't say anything about it.

The trunk popped open and a bright light filled the congested space we were in and two figures blurred into focus. One aimed a revolver while the other reached in and gripped you under the armpits and yanked you out so that your back smacked the asphalt and you squirmed, arched your pelvis at the sky, feeling that sting at the base of your spine. Then the same pair of hands reached inside the trunk and delivered me to the ground by your side. We were on some desolate county road, pocked with potholes. Trees lined either side of the road. Rivera took out a knife and cut the tape around our ankles and said, "Get up," making a rising motion with his hand. Pretty Boy gripped the revolver, kept it fixed on us as we pushed up to our feet, leaning against each other for leverage. He must have noticed how both of us were squinting against the glint of the steel barrel, because he kind of tilted it sideways – as if showing off the merchandise – and said, "Looks like a bitch pistol, huh? Just a .22 mag, like what your momma carries." He grinned with one side of his face. "It'll drop a coyote with one shot, point blank." He squeezed one eye shut, took aim at our faces. "Think your skull is thicker than a coyote's?"

Rivera had retrieved a shovel from the backseat and stood with the spade against his shoulder, watching, letting the young shooter have his fun with us. It was so quiet, I could hear both of our hearts beating.

At some point, Pretty Boy laughed to himself, and Rivera nodded towards the woods, said, "Let's go," and so we did – we walked into the woods to be executed.

Sunlight fractured through the forest ceiling, painting shadows of limbs and branches on our faces. Your eyes darted in every direction as we trudged across the dirt floor. The tape across our mouths wrinkled with each breath in, stretched smooth with each breath out. I couldn't swat at the mosquitos, the way my wrists were taped up. The little shits plunged into my arms and neck and grew plump and buzzed away in swerving patterns, drunk off my blood.

Pretty Boy kept his focus on the backs of our heads, where the bullet holes would go. He held the revolver parallel with his thigh, barrel pointed down, finger caressing the trigger.

Rivera carried a shovel and a bag of Cheetos. He shook the chips out of the bag into his mouth. Chewed with his mouth open.

"There's javelinas in these woods," he said. "When the people in town hear the gunshots, they'll say to themselves, 'good riddance,' and they won't realize they're talking about you." He shook more chips into his mouth.

You had fixated on something up ahead. You looked at me and then looked straight again, directing my attention with your eyes. I saw where the terrain sloped, and where the top half of a tree lay across the ground, giant splinters jutting out of where it'd been snapped in half by lightning or whatever. Something rustled in the brush nearby – our one shot coming up. You nodded. We dipped.

Pretty Boy shot twice at the javelina rooting in our path and by that time, we had ducked around the fallen timber and split, kept running, not daring to look back.

There was the thunder crack of another shot and the ground in front of us spat dirt in the air.

My prosthetic wasn't the running type. My stride resembled something like an awkward limp in fast forward. You kept looking back at me over your shoulder, screaming through the tape over your mouth. We weaved between trees.

Another thunder crack. The splintered bark of an oak tree grazed my arm.

I stepped wrong and fell forward. You skidded on your heels and dropped to your knees beside me and together we clambered to the top of a levee and took shelter behind a tree. The ground ahead of us took a ten-foot dip to a shallow creek. This is where we would either turn the tables or go down swinging.

The straps on my prosthetic had come undone. The left knee of my jeans bulged in an odd shape. You looked at it and mumbled "what the fuck" beneath the tape.

We could hear the steady pace of approaching footfalls. Crunching leaves, snapping twigs. The sound of bullets clanking against each other and then steel sliding against steel. Pretty Boy had reloaded.

You peeked around the tree. Slammed the back of your head against the trunk and sighed. Your expression said they were closing in.

I slipped my pants off and finished unbuckling the strap around my thigh and offered you my leg. You looked at me sideways with one eyebrow raised. I gripped the steel rod and smacked the thickest part of the prosthetic against the ground. You nodded your head up and down and took the leg in both hands and stood with your back against the tree. Watched out of the corner of your eye for a head to pop up.

You saw your moment, but it was a matter of distance, I guess. Pretty Boy wasn't going to get close enough without seeing us first, so might as well go the "fuck it" route and do something unexpected, like leap out from the cover of one tree to another, wielding a fake leg like a baseball bat, ducking two gunshots, coming out from around a tree with the leg raised skyward, bringing it down hard enough against the side of Pretty Boy's head to send him spinning and shooting blindly on his way to the ground. You dropped the leg and put your knees in his chest and – since your wrists were still bound — you interlocked your fingers and went to swinging at his face with both fists serving as one. Each blow echoed, sounded like raw meat slapping concrete.

And there I was, crawling across the dirt in my boxers, searching for a rock with a sharp enough edge.

And there was Rivera, charging out from behind a bush with a shovel raised over his head, veins bulging in his face.

And there I was again, too late to do anything.

The spade caught your chin, sent you rolling sideways. I crawled frantically in your direction, not sure of what to do, logic replaced by rage and the fear of losing you. Rivera raised the shovel again, sharp tip of the spade aimed at your neck, and caught a bullet in the chest, then another in the throat. My eyes shook. This scene was playing out like a fucked up film reel, the image frozen, stuttering. There was Pretty Boy lying on his back, coughing up his teeth, the bones in his face rearranged so the tattoo above his eyebrow was now a thing of irony.

There was Rivera, spitting blood from the hole in his neck, crimson circles growing on his shirt.

And there you were, on your back with the smoking .22 in your grip, still pulling the trigger, the empty chambers clicking and rotating.

The shovel fell to the ground, and Rivera followed.

I crawled up next to you and put my hands over yours and you lowered the gun. I went to pull the tape off your mouth – your skin stretching with it, until I got to your lips, ripped it the rest of the way off in one quick tug. You ripped mine off with zero attempt at delicacy and I hollered.

You shrugged, said, "My bad." You pulled the shovel over to you by the spade and slipped the edge between your wrists to cut the tape off and then I did the same. I crawled over to my leg and tied it back on. Stood and leaned against a tree.

You sat, catching your breath. You said, "Hey."

I said, "What."

You said, "Run his pockets."

I dug around in Rivera's pockets, found a switchblade, keyring, cell phone, and a thick wad of hundred dollar bills rolled up and rubber banded together. I tossed the loot into your lap and you counted out the cash, said, "Bruh." You said, "We got rent money."

Pretty Boy moaned. His eyes fluttered open, his vision tinted red by the blood that flowed from his broken nose. I sat on his chest and gripped his throat in my hands. He thrashed about and slapped at the air in front of my face and I tightened my grip and for a second, his face changed, became the face of our pit bull Gorgeous, and I clenched my eyes shut and the tears fell but I didn't let go until I felt his body go limp.

We took turns digging the hole to roll the bodies in. You tamped the dirt flat with the spade. A blood red moon filled what we could see of the sky through the trees. Cicadas chirped. We fell against a tree and caught our breath. Some time passed and then we stood and picked a direction to walk in.

We knelt down in the muddy bank of a creek and washed the blood from our hands, our forearms, our elbows. You took off your shirt and held it in the current and the water turned dark.

You rung out the wet shirt, tied it around your neck, said, "I think we're going the wrong way."

I studied the tree line. The shadows moving within the shadows. Pointing in no particular direction – just somewhere different than where we'd come from, and from where we were now – I said, "Let's go this way," and we were walking again.

The air was a sticky kind of warm. Things rustled in the dark – snakes and armadillos and whatever creatures the glowing eyes belonged to.

You stopped and touched my shoulder with your fingertips in a way that paralyzed me instantly. We stood frozen. You said, "You see that?" and I didn't know what you meant at first but then, yeah, I saw it: how the shadows bent and the darkness took on a new shape, and I'm glad we were both there to see it, how this new shape in the dark – how it looked like Moms standing there.

*I heard you scream before I opened my eyes.*

The crown of chaotic curls atop her head made her unmistakable, even beneath the shadows of the trees. A shimmer of crimson moonlight shone across her neck and collarbone.

You said, "I can't feel my legs," and I caught you by the armpit before you could collapse. Draped your arm across my shoulders. A chill breeze flowed between us and I felt your ribs vibrate against mine. Sweat rolled from your eyes and you bit your lip. Both of our gazes were transfixed on the apparition.

She cut through the trees and we followed. Your knees wobbled and your shoes dragged across the cracked dirt as I held you upright and shuffled forward on one good leg. Overhead, branches interlocked like fingers, blacking out the sky. We came to a small clearing where a sliver of copper-tinted moonlight beamed down, and the ghost of Moms paused inside of the luminescence for a moment – tilted the side of her head in our direction – the faint presence of a smile at the corner of her mouth.

*Nurses carried us to a blanket spread out on a cold, metal table. They set us next to each other and toweled the blood and birth cheese off our bodies.*

Before we could catch up to her beneath the red moon, she was moving forward again, almost floating across the ground.

*"You okay back there, babies?"*

The ghost slipped further into the shadows as we struggled to keep up and eventually, we heard motors humming, saw headlights cutting through the trees. We were almost out of the woods.

Kelby Losack is the author of *Heathenish* and
*Toxic Garbage*. He lives with his wife in Gulf Coast Texas.
One of these days, he'll quit fucking around
and drop a fire mixtape.


Twitter: @HeathenishKid

Much love and gratitude to J. David Osborne, for caring about my shit as much as I do, and for all the phone calls. Broken River for life.

To Donald Glover for creating *Atlanta*.

To my brothers and sisters in the indie writing scene. Keep up the hustle (except the fuckheads —you know who you are—you're welcome to stop).

To the artists I listened to while writing this: JPEG-MAFIA, Night Lovell, AzSwaye, WiFi Gawd, Kent Loon, Chester Watson, Bones, Danny Brown, Retch, Derek Wise, Blvc Svnd, L0RD_B1LE, Lo$ Zvfiro$, Shoreline Mafia, Vince Ash, Haleek Maul, and Lil Ugly Mane.

And most of all to Erika—my wife, my love, my Queen of Swords. I'd be lost without your support.

Find more information on Broken River Books at:


www.brokenriverbooks.com


Listen to Kelby on episode 113 of The JDO Show at:


www.thejdoshow.podbean.com

38431643R00060

Printed in Great Britain
by Amazon